Cottage
Barn

EGMONT

We bring stories to life

First published in Great Britain in 1991 by Heinemann Young Books
imprints of Egmont Children's Books Limited
239 Kensington High Street, London W8 6SA.
Published in hardback by Heinemann Library,
a division of Reed Educational and Professional Publishing Limited
by arrangement with Egmont Children's Books Limited.
This edition published 2010 by Egmont UK Ltd
239 Kensington High Street, London W8 6SA
Text copyright © Michael Morpurgo 1991
Illustrations copyright © Ian Andrew 1999
The Author and Illustrator have asserted their moral rights.
ISBN 978 1 4052 02 558
10 9 8 7 6 5 4 3 2 1
A CIP catalogue record for this title
is available from the British Library.
Printed at Oriental Press Limited, Dubai.

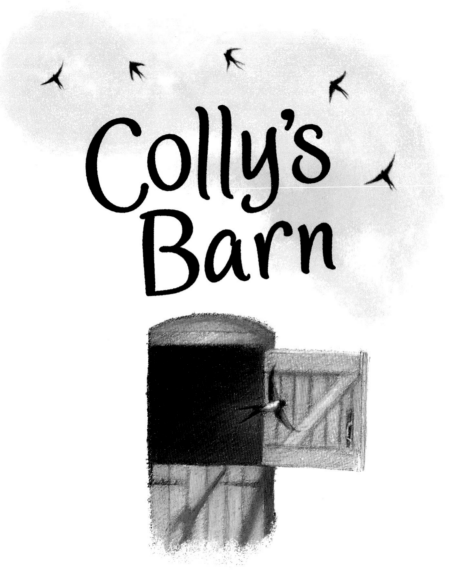

Colly's Barn

MICHAEL MORPURGO

Illustrated by Ian Andrew

Red Bananas

For Catherine, Simon, Jonathan,

Susannah and James

M.M.

To the memory of

Phil O'Connor

I.A.

Chapter One

SOMEONE HAD TO clean out the old barn.
Grandad had a bad knee and her mother and
father were busy, so Annie had to do it all by
herself. But she wasn't alone. You were never
quite alone in the old barn.

Screecher, the barn owl, looked down at her
from his perch on the beam above her. She
knew that the swallows would be watching her
from their nests high on the roof joists. But the
owls and the swallows were as much a part of
the barn as the mud walls and the thatched
roof and she paid them no attention.

It was hot work and smelly too, but Annie
was used to that. After all she had grown up
on a farm and on a farm there were always
smells of one kind or another. This was no
worse than most.

'Be nice if the cows would learn to clean up
after themselves,' said Grandad from the door

of the barn. 'I thought maybe you could do
with some water.' They sat down side by side
on a hay bale. Annie drank till the bottle was
empty. Grandad was looking around him. 'This
barn, your father wants to knock it down you
know,' he said.

'What for?' said Annie.

7

'Old fashioned, he says, and maybe he's right.'
Grandad prodded the wall with his stick. 'Cob
that is, just mud, a few stones, straw; and it's
lasted all that time. Course there's a few cracks
in it here and there, but I told your father, it'll
go on for a few years yet.'

On the beam above them Screecher stretched
his legs and flexed his talons. Grandad looked
up. 'And Screecher, he's been here since the
place was built, or his family has. Always nest
in the same place they do. Same as those
swallows, they've been coming here ever since
I can remember.' Grandad stood up and leaned
on his stick. 'Makes you think,' he said, 'thousands

9

of miles they come every year, across
African deserts, over the sea, and straight back
to this barn. There's one now.' As he spoke
Colly flew in over his head and up to the nest
above, fluttered there for a moment and then
swooped down again and out of the door.

'Look,' said Annie, 'there's a
baby in the nest, you can
see its head.'

'So you can,' said
Grandad. 'You can hear
it too. I wonder what it's
saying.'

Annie laughed. 'Birds
don't talk,' she said.

'Not like you maybe,' Grandad said, 'and not like me, but they talk all right. We just don't understand what they're saying, that's all. I wonder if they understand us?'

'Course not,' said Annie, but it gave her a lot to think about while she mucked out and when you've got something to think about time passes quickly. She never even noticed the evening coming on and she never once looked up at the swallows' nest again. If she had, she'd have seen the fledgling swallow perched precariously on the edge of its nest trying out its wings.

Screecher saw it but did not say anything. Colly was a good mother. She did not need any advice from him as to how to bring up her

family. She was his friend too, his oldest friend. They'd been living in the barn longer than any of the other birds. All winter, every winter, he would look forward to the day when Colly would come flying back into

the barn, bringing the spring with her. And when she arrived she never rested, not for a moment. She'd be building her nest, working every hour of the daylight. She'd hatch out her eggs and then she'd be flying in and out, in and out, keeping her family fed, and this year she'd had to feed them all on her own. No one really knew what had happened to her mate. He just went off hunting one morning and never came back. It could have been a car; it could have been a cat.

13

Screecher was just thinking about the cat when he heard her, and then he saw her creeping in through the door. Everyone warned everyone else. 'Look out! Look out!' they cried as the cat stalked stiffly past the hay bale and sat down under Colly's nest, her tail whisking to and fro, her eyes fixed on the nest above her.

Screecher knew what would happen, he'd seen it all too often before.

Suddenly terrified, Colly's last fledgling beat his wings frantically. Then he overbalanced and fell. The cat watched as he fluttered helplessly down towards the floor of the barn. She knew she had only to wait. There was no hurry, no hurry at all. She wasn't even hungry, she'd already had a nest of mice that day. This bird was for playing with.

At that moment Colly
came gliding in, a
mayfly in her beak.
She dived at once,
screaming at the
cat, banked steeply
and came in again.
The cat ducked as
Colly flashed by and
she swiped the air with an
unsheathed claw as she passed
overhead. The fledgling was flapping his way
to the corner of the
barn. The cat
crawled after him,
belly on the
ground, ignoring
Colly's desperate
attempts to drive
her off.

There was
only one thing
Colly could do.

She landed between the cat and her stranded fledgling and hopped away on a leg and a wing pretending to be wounded. 'I've broken it.' she cried. 'I've broken my wing.'

The cat stopped, turned and followed her. A big bird was always better sport than a small bird.

Screecher sprang off his perch and floated down on silent wings. The cat heard the whisper of wind through Screecher's feathers and looked up. She saw the spread white wings and the talons coming at her, open and deadly. She backed away in surprise. Screecher had never challenged her before.

'Colly,' said Screecher, keeping his eyes on the cat as she slunk away. 'I'm going to pick him up and put him back in the nest. Tell him to hold still. Tell him not to be frightened.'

His talons curled carefully under and around the fledgling. Then he took off, lifting him higher and higher until at last he was hovering above the nest and could let him go. The fledgling dropped down into the nest and huddled, complaining, in a corner. Colly landed beside him. 'I told you you weren't ready to fly yet, didn't I? I told him, Screecher. Wait till your wings are stronger, I said. Wait till tomorrow. But they don't listen.'

Screecher shivered. 'I think there's a storm
coming,' he said. 'I can feel it in the wind. I'd
best be off hunting before the rain comes,' and
he opened his wings and lifted off the beam.

'Screecher,' Colly called after him. 'Thanks a
million. I won't forget it, not ever.'

'What are friends for?' said Screecher as he
floated away out through the barn door and
into the dusk.

The road was always the best hunting ground. The hedgerows on either side were full of rustling voles and mice and rats. He had a good night of it. Five kills he made, but his two scrawny owlets just ate and asked for more. The rumble of thunder was coming dangerously close now. He'd been caught out in a storm once before. Once was enough. 'I'm telling you, you can't go hunting with wet feathers,' he told them, but that didn't stop them from grumbling on about how hungry they were.

Chapter Two

ALL NIGHT, AS the storm raged outside, the birds in the barn huddled together in their nests, burying their heads in each other to blot out the sound of the thunder. The wind whined and whistled through the eaves, the walls shuddered and the beams creaked and groaned. But Screecher and Colly were not worried. They'd been through storms like this before and the old barn had held together.

Screecher thought the worst of it was over. He was peering through a crack in the wall, looking for the first light of dawn on the

distant hills, when the lightning struck. In one
blinding flash night was turned to day. A
deafening clap of thunder shook the barn and a
fireball glowing orange and blue rolled around
the barn and disappeared through the door.

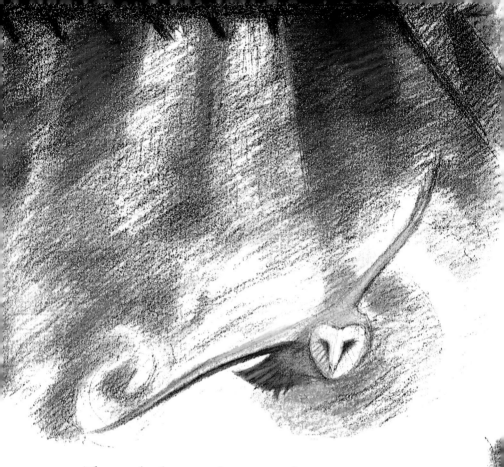

Through the smoke Screecher could see that
the crack in the wall was suddenly a gaping
hole and above him the roof was open to
the rain.

Grandad's bad knee kept him in bed the next
morning and Annie was at school when her
father and mother discovered the hole in the
barn wall.

'Lucky it didn't catch fire,' said Annie's mother.

'Might have been better if it had,' said her father. 'One way or another that barn's got to come down now. I've been saying it for years.'

'You could patch it up,' Annie's mother replied.

Her father shook his head. 'Waste of time and money. New modern shed, that's what we need. I'll have a bulldozer in, we'll soon have it down.'

'Grandad won't like it,' she said. 'You know how much he likes the old buildings. I don't want you upsetting him again.'

'It's just a tumbledown old barn,' he said.
'Anyway, Grandad won't know till it's all over.
He won't be out of bed for a couple of days,
not with his knee like it is. And not a word to
Annie, she tells him everything. Thick as thieves
they are, those two.'

High above them in the old barn, Screecher
and Colly were perched side by side listening
to every word. 'What'll we do?' said Screecher.
'There's nowhere else to nest for miles around;
and even if there was, my two children won't

be ready to fly for another month or more. I can't move them and I won't leave them. I won't.'

Colly said nothing. She flew off to join the swifts and housemartins as they skimmed low over the high grass in Long Meadow. The message that Screecher and his family were in trouble soon got around. At first some of them refused to help. There was a rumour that Screecher had killed a cock robin not so long ago. The sparrows and the crows, and there were a lot of them, said that it was nothing to do with them, that everyone had to look after themselves. But all the birds that lived in the barn, the fan-tailed doves, the swallows, the swifts, and the little wren, needed no persuading. After all they'd seen Screecher, only the day before, diving down to rescue Colly's fledgling from the cat.

'I've got babies in my nest just like Screecher,' said the wren. 'And anyway, if they knock down the barn where are we going to nest next year and the year after that?'

All day long the birds argued, and it was almost dark before they were all agreed at last. 'Then we'll start work at first light tomorrow,' said Colly. 'Let's all get some sleep.'

Chapter Three

THE NEXT MORNING Grandad looked out from his bedroom window at the crowd of birds swirling around the barn. 'They must be after the flies in the thatch,' he said to Annie's mother when she brought him his early morning tea.

'Who knows,' she said. 'You just stay in bed and rest that knee of yours.'

Annie sat down to breakfast in the kitchen. 'There's swarms of birds out there,' she said. 'Like bees. What're they up to?'

'Who knows,' said her father. 'Eat up, you'll be late for school.'

As she got off the school bus that afternoon Annie could see the birds still soaring and swooping around the barn. She ran up the lane to get a closer look. Grandad was there in his dressing-gown. 'I wouldn't have thought it possible,' he said. 'You see that hole in the wall? Must have happened in the storm. They're mending it, that's what they're doing.'

As Annie watched she saw the swifts and swallows and housemartins come flying in with mud in their beaks. They fluttered briefly at the

wall and flew off again. The crows and
buzzards hovered over the roof before landing
with their twigs and straw, and the wren darted
to and fro, her beak full of moss and lichen.
'Your father's not going to believe this,' said
Grandad.

And he was right. He didn't. Nor did her
mother. They wouldn't even come out to look.

'You'll catch your death, Grandad,' Annie's
mother said. 'Back to bed with you now.'

Annie tried to tell them but they wouldn't
listen to her either. They didn't want to hear
another word about the barn or the birds, not
one word.

'You'll tire yourself out, Colly,' said Screecher that night.

'Don't you worry,' Colly said. 'These wings have taken me to Africa and back five times now, they'll carry me a lot further yet. A few more days and the barn will be as good as new again and then they won't need to knock it down, will they?'

'We need more help with the roof,' said Screecher. 'I'll fly down to the river tomorrow and ask the herons. They're the experts.'

But Colly didn't even hear him, she was fast asleep.

Chapter Four

ANNIE WANTED TO be quite sure Grandad
was right, so all weekend she stayed and she
watched the birds flying back and forth. Even
Screecher was out flying by day and she'd
never seen that before. He was fetching and
carrying just like all the others. Of all of them
though, it was the swallows, and one of them
in particular, that worked hardest, swooping
down to the muddy puddles and up to the
barn wall with never a pause for rest. Annie
knew now for certain that Grandad had not
been imagining things.

'It's true,' she said. 'What Grandad says, it's
all true.' But they still wouldn't believe her.
When she shouted at them she was sent off
to bed early. Grandad came to comfort her.

'There's none so blind as them that won't see,' he said. Annie wasn't sure what he meant by that.

He told her one of his hobgoblin stories, but she could think only of Screecher and the birds in the barn.

She wasn't at all surprised then to see Screecher fly into her dream. He flew in through the window and perched on the end of her bed. There was something in his beak. He let it fall

on her bedcover. She sat up to get a closer
look. It was a dead swallow.

'He's going to knock down the barn,' said
Screecher.

'Who is?' said Annie.

'Your father. We heard him, Colly and me.'

'Colly?'

'That's Colly lying on your bed,' Screecher
said. 'I tried to tell her, I told her she'd kill
herself if she worked so hard. She never stopped
– all day and every day. We've got to finish it,
she said, and then they won't have to knock
down our home.'

'Home?' said Annie.

'That barn is our
home. We've got
nowhere else to live.
You've got to stop him.
You've got to tell your
father or else he'll
bring in the bulldozer.'

'But he won't believe me,' said Annie. 'He
doesn't believe anything I say. You tell him.
He'll believe you, he'll listen to you.' And
Screecher was suddenly gone.

It's a funny thing about dreams, they always
seem to finish just as you wake up. There was

a rumbling outside
Annie's window, and
voices. She sat up and
looked out. Her father
was standing by a
great yellow bulldozer
that belched black
smoke and he was
pointing up at the

barn. Annie looked down and saw the swallow lying on her bed. She picked it up. Colly was limp in her hand, her beak half open. Annie never bothered with slippers or her dressing gown. She ran crying out of the house. Grandad heard her and her mother heard her. Her father heard nothing until the driver of the bulldozer switched off his engine and pointed at Annie as she came running up the path. Her father looked at the swallow in her hand.

'That's Colly isn't it?' he said.

Annie looked at him amazed. 'You know?' she said.

'I had a visitor last night,' he said. He told me everything, Annie. He brought me out here to show me the hole they'd mended. When I woke up this morning I thought I'd been sleepwalking, so I came and had another look. I wasn't dreaming, Annie.'

'Neither was I,' said Annie.

Grandad came puffing up the path, with
Mother behind him. 'What's going on?' said
Grandad. 'What's that bulldozer for?'

'Oh, nothing,' said Annie's father. 'Just took
a wrong turning somewhere, that's all. Lost his
way. We all do that from time to time, don't we
Grandad?'

They buried Colly that morning in the
corner of Long Meadow under the great ash
tree. If Annie had looked up she'd have seen
Screecher perched high above her, half hidden
by the leaves, Colly's fledgling beside him.
And they weren't alone. Every branch,
every twig of the tree was lined with
silent birds.